This edition published by Parragon Books Ltd in 2017 and distributed by

Parragon Inc.
440 Park Avenue South, 13th Floor
New York, NY 10016
www.parragon.com

ISBN 978-1-4748-6869-3

Printed in China

One day in Metropolis, Clark Kent went to interview the police chief. But when Clark arrived at the station, he knew something was wrong. All the police officers were standing around their office, completely still. Nobody moved! One of the officers looked at Clark with a strange, blank stare.

"I know that look," said Clark. He turned the officer around and, just as Clark had suspected, there was a small starfish stuck to the back of his neck.

Clark checked each officer—they all had a starfish!

"Starro!" he cried.

Clark knew he had to act fast.

"This looks like a job for Superman!"

Superman had faced Starro before. The evil alien starfish could take over anyone's mind. He was a very powerful enemy, and this time, Starro had even more people under his control!

Superman needed help, so he called his friends Batman and Wonder Woman. Starro had struck their cities, too!

"Starro has cloned himself and sent his
legion to destroy our cities," said Batman.
"To stop him, we'll need help!"
Wonder Woman knew who to call.

Just a few minutes later, Superman, Batman, and Wonder Woman were with some new friends—The Flash, Aquaman, Martian Manhunter, and Green Lantern.

The Flash could run faster than anyone on Earth. Aquaman had the power to swim deep into the ocean without ever getting tired. Martian Manhunter could read people's thoughts. And with his power ring, Green Lantern could create anything he could imagine.

"This is a big job," said Superman. "We must defeat the clones in each of our cities, and then we have to find Starro and stop him for good." The super heroes agreed to split up into teams.

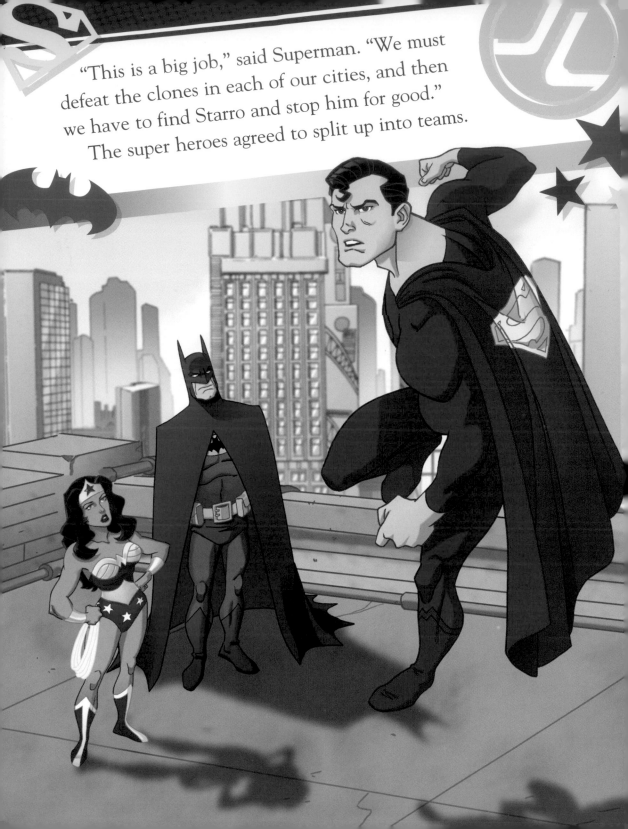

Superman and The Flash zoomed back to Metropolis. The police officers that Starro had brainwashed were all over the city!

"I'll round them up," said The Flash.
"Be back in a second."
In the blink of an eye,
The Flash returned with
all the police officers!

Superman breathed in deeply. Then he froze the starfish on the backs of the officers' necks one by one with his icy breath. The Flash circled around and gathered the frozen clones.

"That was quick," the two speedy super heroes laughed together.

The Flash and Superman raced to
Gotham City. Batman had located all
the clones there with his Batcomputer.
Thanks to The Flash's speed, Superman's
freeze breath, and Batman's combat skills,
they had the clones collected in no time.

Meanwhile, in Washington, D.C., Green Lantern used his power ring to find and gather the brainwashed police officers. Wonder Woman snared one in her Lasso of Truth.

"We'll see about that," said Wonder Woman. "Martian Manhunter, do you copy?" she asked in her mind.

"Got it," said Martian Manhunter. He and Wonder Woman had linked their minds.

"Time to hit the beach," the alien hero told Aquaman.

Martian Manhunter sent the rest of the super heroes a mental message. They all met at the edge of the ocean. Aquaman dived into the water and swam as fast as a shark. There, in the murky depths of the ocean, he found the evil starfish.

Aquaman grabbed Starro by an arm, and pulled him up to the surface. Green Lantern used his ring to help lift Starro out of the ocean, and then Superman froze the villain with his icy breath.

"Time to get rid of this pest," said Martian Manhunter.

He and Superman grabbed Starro and the clones and flew them to outer space. Superman used his super-breath to scatter the starfish all over the galaxy!

Back on Earth, the super heroes celebrated. "Nothing like teamwork to keep the planet safe!" Batman said.